Q. SAVES THE SUN

By Isaac Perry

Illustrations by Shomari Harrington

PARADOX MEDIA PRESS   TIGER STRIPE PUBLISHING

CHICAGO

Dedicated to Paris and Qassim for inspiring Q and fulfilling our dreams.

QSAVESTHESUN.COM

PUBLISHED BY

PARADOX MEDIA PRESS
CHICAGO
PARADOXMEDIA.NET

TIGER STRIPE PUBLISHING
CHICAGO
TIGERSTRIPEPUB.COM

ISBN 978-0-9905895-2-5

25 24 23 22 21 20 19 18 17 16 1 2 3 4 5

Printed in the United States

First printing, September 2016

Cover illustrations by Shomari Harrington. Design by Shawn Hazen.

My name is **Qadeer Taylor**.
Everyone calls me **"Q"**.

Most kids hate when it's bedtime, but not me.

That's because every night my dad sends me on a mission.

And I get to enter a whole new world...

My dad is a motorman for Chicago's train system.

That means he gets to drive the "L" straight through downtown!

Even though he doesn't get home from work until it's almost time for me to go to bed, seeing my dad come home at night is the best part of my day!

Tonight, just like every night, my dad describes a dream to me.

It's always some incredible place he asks me to journey to, or better yet, **an adventure he wants me to go on**.

"Ok, Q," Dad says, "tonight you're an intergalactic space traveler. While you and your crew are out exploring the universe, you discover there's a race of alien robots trying to steal the sun!"

Once the lights go out, I close my eyes.
And the adventure begins...

...and I become **SUPER-Q**: fearless adventurer and space explorer!
Along with my faithful sidekick, **BRIAN the Tyrannosaurus Rex**,

I accept the missions my father gives me and face new villains each and every night!

As our heroes Super-Q and Brian the Tyrannosaurus Rex begin their expedition into the darkest reaches of the cosmos, a terrible sight comes into view…

"There, Brian!" Super-Q shouts. "Those treacherous aliens have already managed to connect their ship to our sun!"

Quickly, Super-Q decides on a daring course of action. "Hit the thrusters, Brian! We'll chase these aliens to the ends of the universe if that's what it takes!"

Just as our courageous explorers dip and dart through the stars, the aliens spot them and accelerate through space.

"The fiends think they've escaped!" Super-Q exclaims.
"But we won't let them succeed. Will we, Brian?"

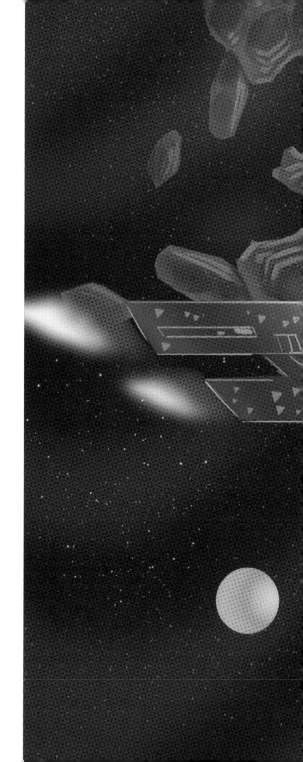

Suddenly, the robots launch an attack!
While laser blasts explode around them, Super-Q gives new orders to his crew.

"Arm the photons, Brian! The sun-thieves know that we are the only thing standing between them and their evil victory. We must defeat these attack jets before the main ship gets away!"

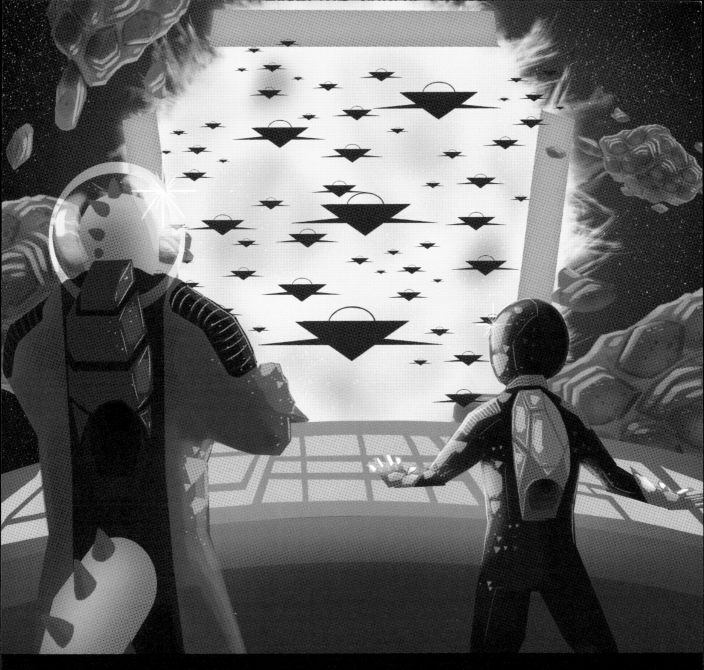

And Brian replies…

"Rawrr!!"

While Super-Q does his best to fight off the space jets,
his ship suffers a terrible hit!

"What happened?
Did our thrusters get hit?"

Brian examines the ship's computer and exclaims,
"Rawrr!!"

"Well," Super-Q replies, "our only hope is to stabilize
the engine and put on our space suits.

It's time to meet these aliens face-to-face!"

Emerging from their damaged ship, Super-Q and Brian prepare to take on the fearsome robot army and save the sun!

Although our heroes fight bravely, Super-Q notices
that their ship has been damaged beyond all repair!

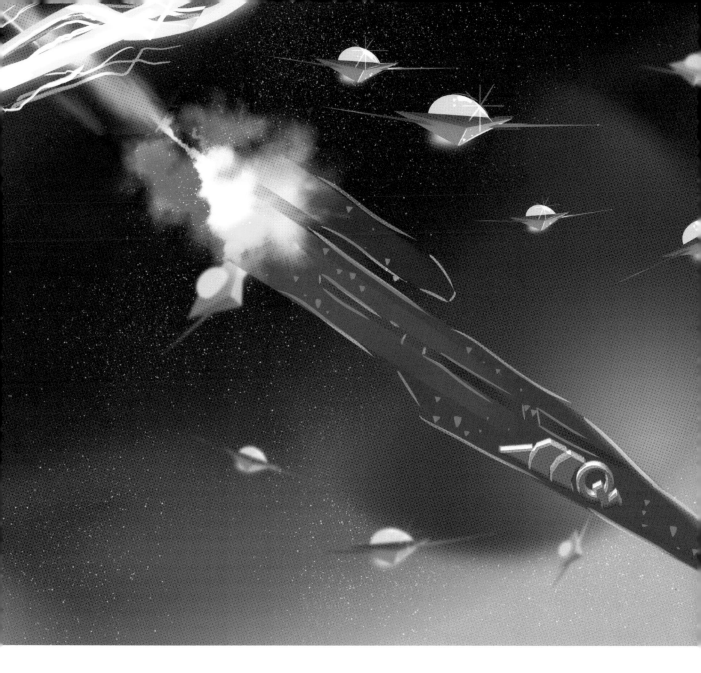

How will he and Brian retrieve the sun and find their
way back to the Milky Way galaxy?

It's then that Super-Q remembers a lesson he learned from his father a long time ago.

The brain is more powerful than the body.
True heroes own powerful *minds*.

"That light," Super-Q thinks.

"It's the same light flashing on all the robot jets, and on the robots themselves."

"Maybe that's what's controlling them?"

27

POW! BAM! Super-Q realizes that reaching the strange, pulsating light may be the key to victory! **CRACK! SMACK!** The robots fight even harder to keep Super-Q and Brian at bay.

BOOM! BAM! But soon the robots realize they chose the wrong
space explorers to mess with!

Finally Super-Q reaches the strange light. "I've only got seconds before those robots overpower us," he thinks.

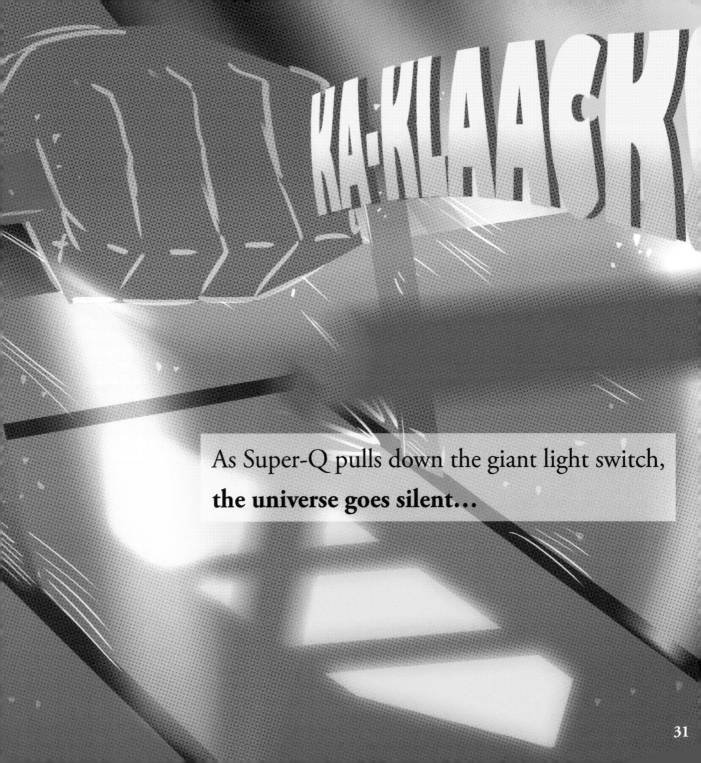

As Super-Q pulls down the giant light switch, **the universe goes silent...**

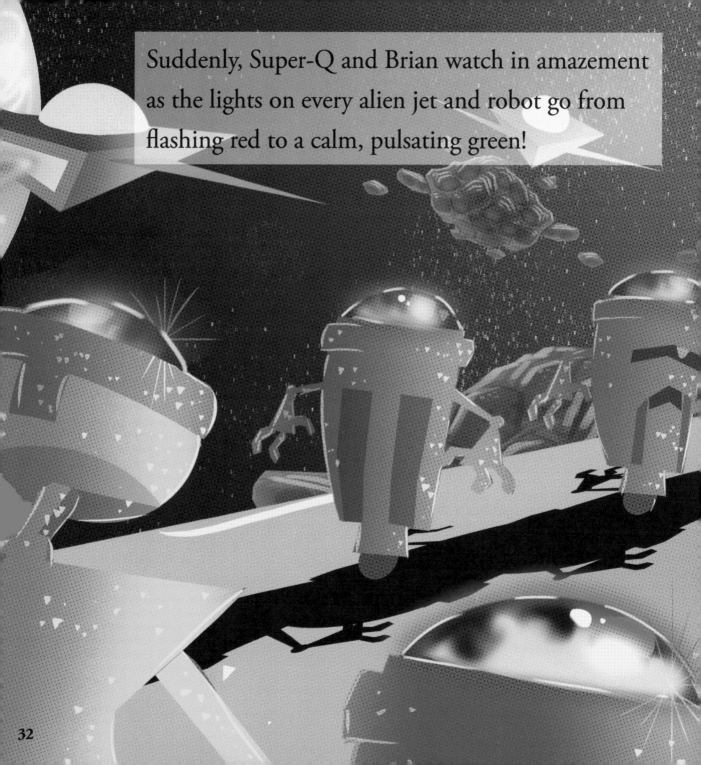

Suddenly, Super-Q and Brian watch in amazement as the lights on every alien jet and robot go from flashing red to a calm, pulsating green!

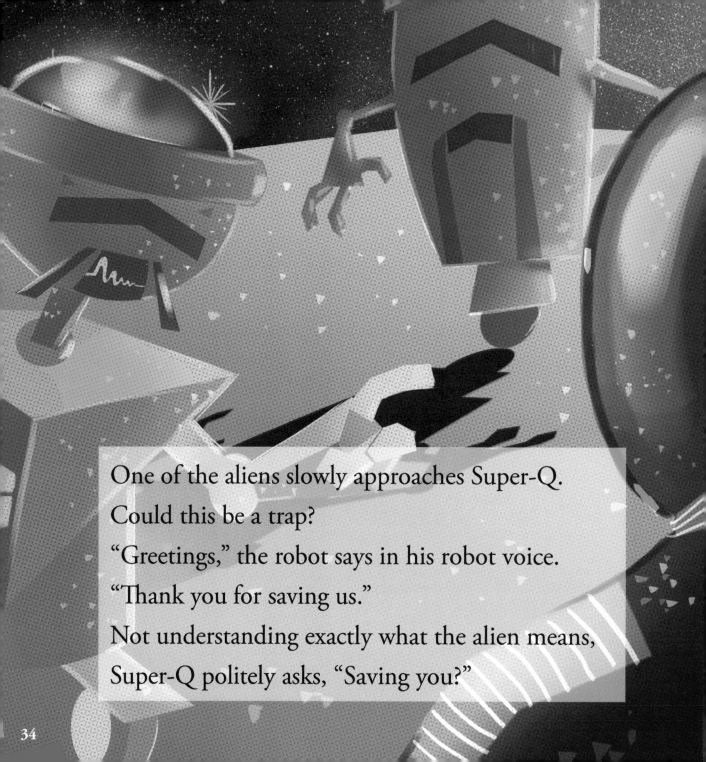

One of the aliens slowly approaches Super-Q.

Could this be a trap?

"Greetings," the robot says in his robot voice.

"Thank you for saving us."

Not understanding exactly what the alien means,

Super-Q politely asks, "Saving you?"

The robot explains, "An evil and powerful alien forced us to steal your sun. He placed that switch on our ship to override our programming.

And then the mighty robot leader says, "But you freed us and we are in your debt! How can we repay you?"

Without any hesitation, Super-Q smiles and tells the alien,
"I think I know *exactly* how you can repay us."

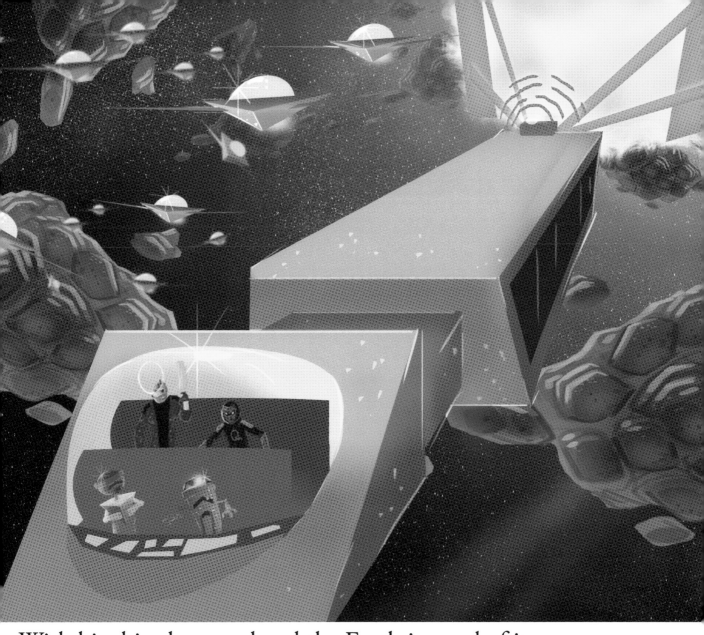

With his ship destroyed and the Earth in need of its sun,
Super-Q requests that the aliens bring the giant yellow star back
to the Milky Way... and give him and Brian a ride home!

Just in time, Super-Q and his new alien friends restore the sun to its rightful place.

"Look, Brian!" Super-Q exclaims. "The sun is back, the Earth is saved, and the robots have been freed! Just another daring exploit to add to the adventures of Super-Q!"

You might have guessed what Brian says...

"Rawrr!!"

Even before my alarm clock goes off I'm reminded that my mission was a success.

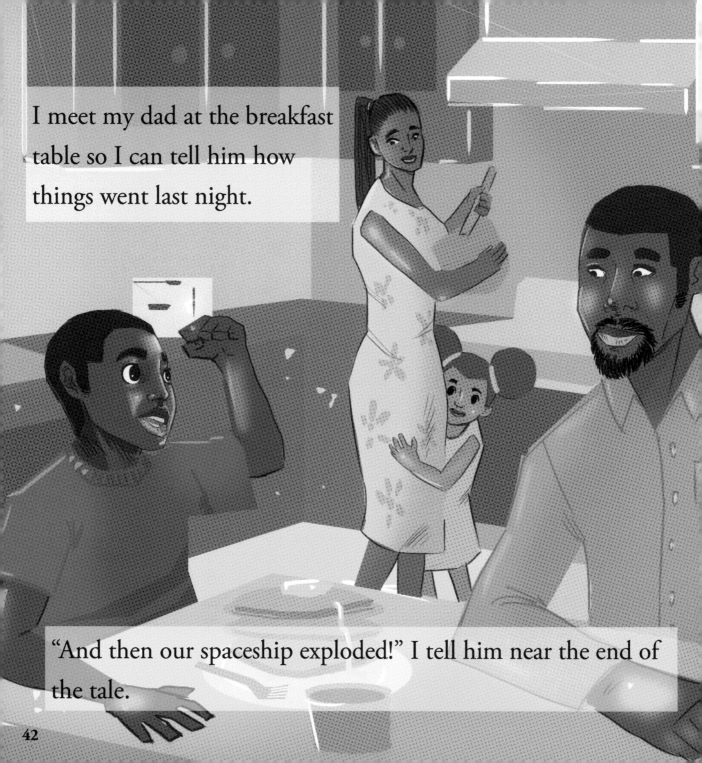

I meet my dad at the breakfast table so I can tell him how things went last night.

"And then our spaceship exploded!" I tell him near the end of the tale.

"What did you guys do then!?" Dad says.

"That's when I noticed the aliens were under mind control and I freed them."

"And then you brought the sun back?" Dad asks.

"Yes, sir," I reply. "Dad, can you imagine what would have happened if everyone woke up and the sun wasn't in the sky?"

"It's a good thing Super-Q and Brian defeated those aliens," my dad says. "That was some battle!"

I smile and say, "That was nothing, Dad. Just wait until tonight…"

Because no matter where the danger may lie, no matter how hard the job may be…

Super-Q and his trusty sidekick, Brian, are always ready for the next great adventure!

CPSIA information can be obtained at www.ICGtesting.com
Printed in the USA
LVIW01n1441250517
535837LV00007B/50